Zoey Finds a Bunny Nest

A Backyard Adventure

Peggy Sue Hentz

Red Creek Wildlife Center, Inc

First edition

Cover design by Peggy Sue Hentz

Illustrations by Peggy Sue Hentz

Author photo © Kathy Miller, www.CelticSunrise.com

ISBN-13: 978-1544795232

ISBN-10: 1544795238

This book is dedicated to

Greg Nason and Kat Hummel

*who have embraced Red Creek's
wildlife rehabilitation mission as their own,
freeing up my time so I can write and teach,
helping even more animals.*

A special thank you to

Allison and Deana Rusinko

*for posing as mother and daughter
for the illustrations.*

Contents

v

A female rabbit searched the yard

to find the perfect spot.

She looked beneath the ivy vine

behind the flower pot.

Here the earth was soft and loose

and hidden out of sight.

The ivy cooled it with its shade;

yes, this spot looked right.

In the darkness of the night

she dug a shallow nest.

She lined it with her belly fur

and then laid down to rest.

That night she had five babies.

Kittens they are called,

although we call them bunnies.

They were helpless, blind and bald.

She cleaned and fed them tenderly

then gently snuck away.

She watched the nest from afar

making sure they were okay.

For five days, undiscovered

she tended to her kits.

She fed and cleaned them through the night

and in the day she hid.

Zoey and her small dog, Max,

loved to play and run.

A lively game of fetch

was always lots of fun.

As hard as she could manage

Zoey threw the ball.

It hit and broke the flower pot

before rolling to the wall.

Max ran into the garden

and stopped sharply in his tracks.

He heard a sudden high-pitched squeal

and pushed the ivy back.

Max dug into the hidden nest

spreading nest fur all about.

He pushed his nose into the hole

and pulled a bunny out.

He quickly ran to Zoey
to show her his new friend,
and gently dropped the bunny
into her open hand.

Max was so excited
and hoping for more fun,
he ran back toward the flowerpot
to grab another one.

Zoey yelled for Max to come.

"No Max! Stay away!

The little bunnies are not toys;

they don't want to play."

Zoey safely tucked the bun

in the pocket of her blouse.

Holding tight to Max's collar

they went into the house.

"Mommy! Mommy, come and see

what Max found by the wall.

I think it's a baby bunny.

It's really, really small."

Zoey slowly pulled the bun

from the pocket of her shirt

and handed Mom the bunny

to see if it was hurt.

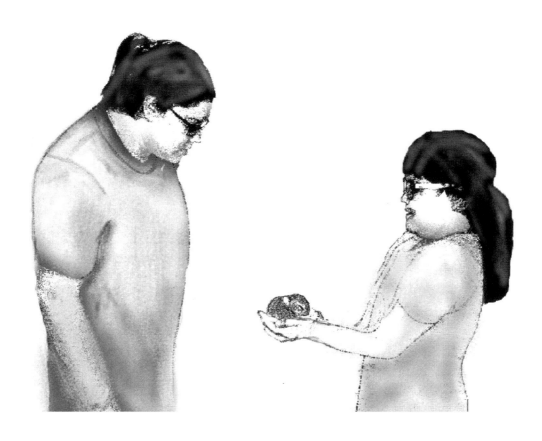

"Mommy can I keep him
and raise him till he's grown?
He's the cutest little bunny
I think I've ever known."

"That's not a good idea.
I don't think it's wise
to try to make a pet
out of something that is wild."

"I know some wildlife folks.
We'll call them right away.
We'll tell them about the bunny
and see what they have to say"

The wildlife center answered

and knew just what to do.

"We help people every day

with problems just like you. "

"Gently take each bunny, and

make sure they're dry and warm.

Look each over, head to tail,

to see if they are harmed. "

"There are no cuts or scratches.

Nothing to be found."

"Then, all the baby bunnies

should be renested in the ground."

"Is it true the rabbit mother
will now abandon them
because Max disturbed the nest,
and we held them in our hands?"

"That's an old wives' tale,
so you need not be alarmed.
The mother won't abandon them
or cause them any harm."

"The mother rabbit is hiding,
but she isn't very far.
They are much better mothers
than we give them credit for."

To make sure she comes tonight,

try this easy test:

you can place an "X" of yarn

atop the bunny nest."

"Can we move the bunnies?

Our dog knows where they are.

He'll go right to the nest

when he's in the yard."

"The rabbit mom won't find them.

She memorized the spot.

She'll only look for her nest

behind the flowerpot."

"Can you keep Max on a leash

or build a fence around,

or when he is out to play,

place a board down on the ground?"

"How long must we do this?

Is it possible to guess?

How long until the bunnies leave?

How long they're in the nest?"

"That shouldn't be hard to do.

Let's try to tell their age.

They grow up so very fast.

Every day they change.

When they're born, their eyes are closed;

they cannot not hear or see.

In as little as a few short weeks

they're ready to go free."

"On day one, they're helpless
with no fur on their backs.
Except for their pink bellies,
they are shiny and all black."

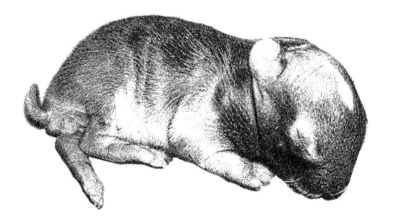

"The second day they start to dull
and their skin is gray as lead.
Day three they start to grow brown fur
on their faces and their heads."

"Day four, they look like rabbits:
they are fully furred and brown.
Day five, they can now sit up
and start hopping all around."

"Day six is a special day
that brings a cool surprise.
When they turn six days old,
they open up their eyes."

"Every day thereafter,

they continue to grow and grow.

By the time they're three weeks old,

they are old enough to go."

"They are jumpy little bunnies,

but their eyes are still shut tight.

So, from what you've said,

five days seem just right."

Zoey and her mother
returned the bunnies to the ground
and gathered up the bunny fur
that Max had thrown around.

They tucked the fur in loosely.
The bunnies snuggled in to hide
behind the broken flowerpot
beneath the ivy vine.

When everything looked finished
they added one last thing.
Overtop the bunny nest,
they laid down the "X" of string.

That night the mother rabbit

snuck back into the yard

like she'd done each night before,

but this time was alarmed.

She saw the nest was different

and was scared her kits were gone

because everything was rearranged.

She ran across the lawn

With frantic speed she moved the fur

and opened up the nest.

With relief she found her bunnies

and moved the string that was the test.

One by one she checked each bun.

All were cleaned and fed.

She pulled out some more belly fur

to softly line their bed.

When all were full and comfortable,

and everything looked right,

she covered the nest to hide it

and snuck away into the night.

Early the next morning

Zoey ran out to check their test.

She just couldn't wait to see

if the string was on the nest,

She saw the string was pulled away,

and she knew from what we learned,

that if that string had moved at all,

Mommy Rabbit had returned.

Zoey promised that she wouldn't,

but she had to take one peek.

They were snuggled deeply in the nest,

and all were fast asleep.

They laid a pallet on the ground

as a protective barrier

that gave room for the rabbit,

but not the happy terrier.

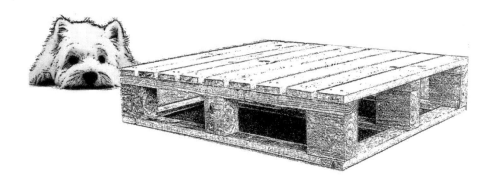

Every day for exercise

Zoey took Max out to the park

where he could play with other dogs,

fetch the ball and run and bark.

Every night mom rabbit returned.

Each day the bunnies grew.

Once, Zoey saw Mom Rabbit

and wondered if she knew

that for two weeks they helped the bunnies

by protecting the nesting spot,

underneath the ivy vine

behind the broken flowerpot.

Two weeks after the nest was found,

the buns began to roam.

Now old enough to leave the nest,

they set out on their own.

One ran for the bushes.

Another stood real still.

Another ran through Zoey's legs

and fell down the window well.

Zoey's mom again stepped in
and put them all into a bin.
She called the wildlife folks
to learn what's next and make a plan.

Now that the buns were old enough
she learned it was not hard
to move them to a safer place
outside of Max's yard

So, life went back to normal
for Zoey and her mom,
and Max got to once again
run freely in his yard.

One night the mother rabbit

returned to Zoey's lawn.

She hopped over by the wall,

and the flowerpot was gone.

It was time for her to nest again.

She was looking for a place,

and she knew because of last time

that Zoey's yard was safe.

She sniffed around the bushes,

along the fence and by the wall.

Then she looked across the yard

and saw the perfect spot of all.

She ran across the garden

and snuck underneath the pine.

The ground here was cool and soft.

Yes, this spot was fine.

That night she had six babies.

Kittens they are called,

although we call them bunnies.

They were helpless, blind and bald.

For Parents

WHAT TO DO IF A BUNNY NEST IS FOUND

"Zoey Finds a Bunny Nest" is more than a wonderful story. It is a life lesson about the most common wildlife encounter experienced by everyone, especially children. Please use this tale to teach children to respect wildlife and to not to interfere with nature.

Cottontail bunnies are the most frequent animal patients in many wildlife rehabilitation centers. In any given year, Red Creek receives over five hundred juvenile cottontails, one-quarter of our total wildlife patients.

Cottontail nests are often exposed following a gardening accident, mowing the lawn, or when suddenly found by a child or a pet.

The discovery of a cottontail nest does not necessarily constitute an emergency or a need for intervention. If the bunnies were not injured, the nest could be returned to its original condition, and the mother will continue caring for the babies.

Because the success rates of rehabilitating young cottontail rabbits are often much lower than those for other species, every effort must be taken to keep bunnies with the mother when possible.

Two misunderstandings about rabbit nests result in excessive interference:

29

First is the belief that the mother will abandon or kill the babies because the nest was disturbed or the babies were touched. This is a fallacy. The mother will NOT abandon or kill her babies. On rare occasions, she might move them, but will most likely just continue caring for them as usual.

The second misunderstanding comes from the finder's not seeing the mother after the nest was discovered, convincing her that the nest was actually abandoned. The mother's absence is part of the fundamental biology and defense of the nest. Understanding the behavior of the mother rabbit and why that behavior works to keep the nest from predators is important for the rehabilitator and should be relayed to the finder.

NESTING BEHAVIOR

The location of the nest is essential to its thriving. The spot chosen often has to do with temperature, humidity, and location of first foods for the bunnies nearby; such as dandelion and clover.

The nest remains clean because the baby bunnies cannot defecate or urinate on their own until they are old enough to leave the nest. When the mother visits the nest to feed the bunnies, she stimulates them and eats the excrement, keeping the nest odor-free.

A nesting bunny's scent glands have not yet developed, and they do not put off an odor of their own. They will remain odorless for much of their juvenile development. They absorb odors around them, becoming odor camouflaged, and blend into the environment.

The mother rabbit does have mature scent glands, however, and leaves a scent wherever she rests. Except for short visits to feed and tend to the kits, she stays away from the nest so her own odor does not linger.

Although human scent at the nest or on the bunnies will not discourage the mother, it is possible to leave enough human scent at the nest so that a predator might get curious and find the nest. For this reason, handling should be minimized to only that which is necessary.

We are often asked if a nest can be moved because of dangers such as those from dogs. The answer is: NO! Because the babies do not put off an odor, even the mother cannot find them if they have been moved.

Nesting rabbits consume massive amounts of milk each feeding. The stomach capacity of young rabbits is two to three times that of most mammal babies, and, therefore, the rabbits require feedings to receive proper nutrition. Newborn bunnies only nurse two to three times in a twenty-four hour period. Within a week, one to two daily feedings is all that is required.

Since the mother's visits are infrequent and brief, her perceived absence results, and a person finding and watching the nest might believe the nest has been abandoned.

TESTING THE NEST

Occasionally an adult rabbit will be found dead near a known nest. The dead adult might or might not be the actual mother. There are two ways that a nest can be tested to determine if the mother is still caring for the babies.

First is the string test which we described in our story. Place two pieces of yarn or string loosely over the nest in the shape of an "X." Because the mother mostly visits at night, this should be done in the early evening. The next morning, check the nest to see if the yarn has been moved. If the nest was untouched, the babies have been orphaned.

Another test is to pick up one or two babies and look at their bellies. In their first week of life, a cottontail's belly skin is very thin and partially transparent. If they've been recently fed, there will be a light-colored triangle in the center of the abdominal area. This is milk in the stomach, revealing that they have been recently fed.

Keep in mind that bunnies slowly digest the milk so this milk can be observed for up to twelve hours. A recheck twelve to twenty-four hours later will assure you that the mother is still returning and has fed the bunnies.

IDENTIFYING EMERGENCIES

All visible injuries are an immediate emergency. Gardening accidents, a nest that has been stepped on, and pet attacks often result in injuries. If a single bunny has been injured, perhaps the remaining rabbits can be left in the nest. If the injury to one bunny has left blood in or near the nest, the entire nest is in danger of failing.

A mower accident will often wound or kill one or two babies, while the others are untouched. The blood from the injured bunnies will attract flies, and these will lay eggs which will hatch into maggots. This endangers the remaining babies.

Maggots and fly eggs may or may not accompany an open wound. This is a sure sign that the animal is in serious trouble. If left untreated, maggots will eat into wet tissue or openings in the skin, causing infection and literally "eat the animal alive." Most people don't realize that maggots DO NOT need an open wound to an animal's body; they need only constant moisture to develop. Maggots will enter the ears, eyes, mouth, and other orifices.

Any bunny that was in a dog's or cat's mouth should be treated with antibiotics. Dogs, and especially cats, carry bacteria in their mouths, including pasterellia. This bacterium is highly infectious to wild animals, especially young rabbits. Untreated, the animal can develop a systemic infection that attacks major organs. Once this happens, the animal will die within a few days, and it is very painful.

These are quick and easy decisions. As soon as I hear "my dog or cat had this animal" my immediate response is "get it to a wildlife rehabilitator right away!"

There are times when nest disruption requires evacuation of all the bunnies. Flooding any time of year, and heavy snowfalls in the spring can be considered a natural disaster for a bunny nest. Construction of an area that removes all of the dirt and ground cover may mean that there is no place to rebuild the nest. These are emergencies. Each year, we also receive bunnies found in soil delivered by truck to a home for landscaping. These are cases where rehabbing the entire nest is a must.

If no emergency exists, every effort must be made to re-nest the bunnies so the mother can care for them. Cottontails are difficult to rehab, yet in nature, this is a hardy, prolific animal. A successfully re-nested litter of bunnies often flourishes.

INDEPENDENCE

Cottontails are independent when they are five inches long, which for most is about 15 to 18 days old. They might remain at or near the nest or wander far. Each individual is different.

At this age, they are still fragile and uncoordinated. They do not run fast and often fall when fleeing danger and so are easily captured by predators. However, their scent glands still have not developed, so they remain odor camouflaged. If they stay still in the right background, they blend in with their surroundings becoming visually camouflaged as well.

Blending in is how they survive, and they will continue to be still, even to the point of allowing a person to pick them up. This lack of escape response is often misidentified as a lack of independence and kidnapping results.

Cottontails of this age can be moved out of areas that are dangerous, such as outside of a fenced dog yard. If moved, they should be placed in a safe area with adequate first foods growing such as dandelion and clover.

Putting a young rabbit under a low-hanging pine tree or in a strong smelling area will quickly mask any human scent on the bunny, thus returning its odor camouflage.

Cottontails, even the juveniles, stress very quickly with handling. When relocating an independent bunny, resist the urge to coddle, pet and nurture it. These actions can result in the rabbit experiencing cardiogenic shock, a potentially fatal condition also known as capture myopathy.

To relocate a rabbit, don't carry it in your hands. Instead, place it into a cardboard box and keep the box closed until you are ready to release the bunny. Walk or drive directly to the location. Avoid unnatural sounds such as loud talking and playing the radio.

IF THEY NEED HELP

If you experience an actual emergency with a wild cottontail or a cottontail nest, please don't try to raise baby bunnies at home. They need an experienced, licensed wildlife rehabilitator to receive proper care. Cottontails are delicate, and they are difficult to rehabilitate. Their needs change daily, as does their diet and regimen of maintenance.

Many websites offer care advice, and much of the information given is entirely wrong.

For example, many sites instruct to feed baby bunnies KMR, a kitten milk replacer. Kitten milk is completely different in composition from cottontail milk and will cause a multitude of growth problems.

Milk composition differs from species to species. Average cottontail milk is composed of 35.2% solids, 12.5% protein and 18.4% fat. It is extremely rich and has a high level of fat for a fast growing herbivore. Kitten milk is formulated for carnivores that develop much slower and is composed of 25.4% solids, 11.1% protein, and only 10.9% fat. Kitten milk doesn't even come close to meeting the nutritional requirements for a cottontail rabbit.

You can find local wildlife rehabilitators quickly by using online search engines: Just type your state and the term "wildlife rehabilitation" in the search box. Calls to your state wildlife agencies, local veterinarians, animal shelters, and even 911 will often have successful results.

While searching for professional help, keep the bunny warm and in a dark and quiet location. Don't give it any food or water. Warmth, dark and quiet are all the temporary help they need.

Since many wildlife rehabilitators don't have the resources to pick up animals, please be prepared to transport the animal or animals to them. And please make a donation if you can. For most rehabilitators, donations are their only source of income to buy supplies and that unique formula that baby bunnies need.

WHY SHOULD WE NOT FEED BABY BUNNIES?

Most baby bunnies that are admitted to rehab clinics are dehydrated to some extent. Many are also in a catabolic state, meaning the body is drawing energy from its tissues, fat and even the muscles.

When a starved animal is suddenly fed carbohydrates, such as when a baby bunny is fed milk, "refeeding syndrome" may occur.

When a bunny is suddenly given food, the body attempts to shift back to food as its source of energy, which can result in fluid and electrolyte imbalances and vitamin deficiencies. Insulin is released, causing salts and electrolytes to move from the blood to the body tissues, leaving dangerously low blood levels.

Although life-threatening, the effects are not immediate. The animal might rally from the sugars and fluid and appear okay, but the body's systems begin to fail in three to five days.

Refeeding syndrome is almost impossible to reverse. Most animals will die. A rehabilitator can attempt to give injectable fluids and vitamins, but the damage is usually done.

Wildlife rehabilitators avoid refeeding syndrome by following strict rehydration regimens prior to the introduction of any food products. Success, however, is reliant on the person who originally finds the bunny resisting the overwhelming urge to feed the bunny before taking it to the rehabilitator.

About the Author

A licensed wildlife rehabilitator since 1991, Peggy Hentz is the founder of Red Creek Wildlife Center, Inc and a member of the Pennsylvania Rehabilitation and Education Advisory Council.

She has developed the certification programs for threatened and endangered species in Pennsylvania, and wildlife capture and transport in Pennsylvania and New Jersey.

Peggy has also developed WildlifeEDU.com which offers training opportunities for wildlife professionals through online classes.

Peggy is the author of "Rescuing Wildlife, A Guide to Injured and Orphaned Animals," a guidebook with instructions of how to safely handle wildlife emergency situations.

"Art has been a hobby all my life, and poetry has been a passion since I wrote my first poem at age nine. I never thought these would be used for anything more than my own private reflection until this book. I hope children and adults will enjoy reading "Zoey Finds a Bunny Nest" as much as I enjoyed writing it."

47756064R00027

Made in the USA
San Bernardino, CA
07 April 2017